# Ernest's Special Christmas

Ernest Series ®

*Ernest's Special Christmas* is part of the Ernest Series.

Barnesyard Books and Ernest are trademarks of Barnesyard Books, Inc.

2003© Laura T. Barnes and Barnesyard Books, Inc.

Book design by Christine Wolstenholme

Published by Barnesyard Books, Inc., Sergeantsville, NJ 08557
www.barnesyardbooks.com

Printed in China

Library of Congress Catalog Card Number: 2003090471

ISBN 0-9674681-3-2

# Ernest's Special Christmas

by Laura T. Barnes

Illustrated by Carol A. Camburn

**BARNESYARD BOOKS**

Sergeantsville, NJ 08557 • www.barnesyardbooks.com

*To the special friends who helped us save Chester on that cold December night.*
*Your unwavering love and determination brought about a true Christmas miracle.*
*– L.T.B.*

*To the Coby Family, and all the special animals that have touched our lives.*
*– C.A.C.*

It was a chilly, sunny day on the farm. Christmas was just a day away.

Ernest, Chester and the other animals knew that Christmas was near.
The wreaths with the red bows were on the pasture gates. The pretty wreaths were put there every year.

Ernest loved Christmas. It was a special time shared with friends and filled with wonderful gifts and surprises.

Ernest's friend Chester was a huge, white, draft horse. Although he was very big, he was kind and gentle.

Chester used to pull the plow to dig the fields for planting. But he was very old now and no longer strong enough to help with farm chores. Chester now spent his days quietly munching on grass in the fields.

Ernest, the little miniature donkey, loved the kind, old, draft horse.

When the tiny donkey and the big horse stood side by side, it made Chester look even bigger.

Even though it was a very cold Christmas Eve, the animals stayed warm with their furry winter coats.

Slowly the skies began to turn gray and it started to snow. The animals looked up as small snowflakes fell from the sky. It looked magical.

"It's going to be a beautiful, white Christmas," thought Ernest.

As the day wore on, the flakes got heavier and a soft blanket of snow started to cover the ground. Ernest decided to make his way back to the stall. His tiny hooves and short legs made walking in the snow hard. He slipped a bit as he headed to the barn for shelter.

The snow kept falling. Soon several inches covered the pasture. Ernest was quite happy in his stall. He munched on hay and sipped water from his bucket. His friends slowly joined him.

As Ernest looked around, he realized that Chester was not in the stall. "Hey, where's Chester?" he asked.

"We haven't seen him," said the cows.

"He's not with us," said the horses.

"We haven't seen him either," chimed the donkeys.

Ernest walked through the stall and looked out the door. It was now snowing very hard.
He couldn't see much. Most importantly, he couldn't see Chester.

Ernest ventured down the ramp to see if Chester was nearby. "Nope, no sign of him," thought Ernest.
"I better go find him. After all it's Christmas Eve. We should all be together."

Ernest looked near the birdhouse, but Chester was not there.

He carefully walked down to the pond, slipping along the way. But Chester was nowhere to be found.

Ernest was worried. "Where can he be?" he wondered.

Slowly, Ernest started to walk up the hill toward the back pasture.

He kept slipping and sliding, but continued to search for his friend.

He bent his head low and carefully walked up the hill.

As he climbed, he heard a noise. He turned and walked toward it.
Suddenly he stumbled on something.

"Ouch!" came a deep voice.

Startled, Ernest stopped.

"Hey, be careful. You're on my leg!" boomed the voice.

Ernest looked down and saw Chester lying in the snow.
He realized that he was actually standing on Chester.

"Chester!" shouted Ernest. "There you are! What are you doing laying in the snow?"

"Oh Ernest, I'm so glad you're here. I stumbled in the snow and fell.
Now I can't seem to get up," explained Chester.

"Well, you have to get up," insisted Ernest. "I barely found you.
You blend right in with the snow! Come inside and get warm. Hurry, because it's Christmas Eve.
We are all gathered together in our stall. We're going to celebrate."

"But I can't get up. I'm tired, and I don't have the strength. You go ahead," urged Chester.

Ernest was worried. He saw that Chester was getting covered up by the snow.
He knew that he had to get Chester back to the safety and warmth of the barn.

"I'm not leaving you here. Come on, get up," encouraged Ernest as he nuzzled Chester.

Chester tried but he did not have the strength to raise himself.
He lowered his head back down with a thump.

Little Ernest realized that he couldn't get Chester back on his feet all by himself.
"I have to get help," Ernest explained to Chester.

Ernest made his way back to the barn as quickly as he could. He explained to the horses that he found Chester and needed their help. Without delay, they followed Ernest back out to the pasture.

"Wait for us!" shouted the cows. "We'll help too."

As quickly as possible the animals followed Ernest through the snowy pasture to reach Chester.
The snow was getting so deep that they had trouble finding him.
They finally saw the big, white horse covered in white snow.

They had to work quickly. It was getting very late and they were worried about their friend who seemed so sad and cold. The horses and cows pushed and nudged at the giant horse's back. Chester strained and tried to get up. But each time they pushed, they were only able to get him part way up before he collapsed back on the ground.

It seemed like an impossible task. Yet Ernest was determined and would not give up. They simply must try harder. But each time they did, Chester could only get part way up and then fell back down.

Ernest turned as he heard something coming through the snow. He saw the other donkeys slipping and sliding through the deep snow toward them.

"We want to help too!" yelled the donkeys. Although the donkeys were smaller than the horses and the cows, Ernest realized they needed everyone's help.

The horses and the cows lined up against Chester's back. The donkeys positioned themselves between them.

"Okay! Push, push!" said Ernest. "Puuussshhh!" he yelled.

The horses, cows and donkeys pushed hard as Chester struggled to get up.
But it was no use. As hard as they tried, it just wasn't enough to help their friend.

Hearing the commotion, several birds appeared. "Hey, we'll help too," offered the birds.
They took pieces of Chester's long, white mane and tail in their beaks and began to pull.
"Wait, let's all work together." instructed Ernest. "Ready, set, go!" he shouted.

Then Ernest joined in as he grabbed Chester's halter and began to pull.
The horses, cows and donkeys pushed while little Ernest and the birds pulled.

Ever so slowly Chester started to rise up.

With all of the pushing and pulling, he finally made it all the way up until he found himself standing.

Exhausted, the animals stopped, stood
back and looked at Chester.

"Whew – you did it. You got me up. I'm
standing!" laughed Chester. "I'm standing! I'm standing!"

"Yea for us!" Ernest cheered. "Yea for us!"
he shouted again.

The horses, cows, donkeys, birds – and especially Chester and Ernest – had tears of joy in their eyes.

Ernest couldn't stop shouting and soon they all chimed in. "We did it! We did it! Yea for us!" The horses and cows trotted around Chester. Ernest and the other donkeys bucked with glee and the birds flew in circles.

Then to their surprise they heard the faint sound of bells off in the distance.
They seemed to be coming from overhead.
The animals had been working so hard, they did not realize that it was already Christmas.

Ernest looked up and smiled at the sound of the bells.

He knew that Christmas is a time of giving.

Ernest felt so proud and joyous that he and his friends were able to help Chester.

With love and determination they had helped their friend.

Now they would all be able to celebrate Christmas together. This was the best gift of all.

It truly was a very, very special Christmas.